SUPER SANDCASTLE
Going Green

WHAT IN THE WORLD IS A GREEN GARDEN?

Oona Gaarder-Juntti

Consulting Editor, Diane Craig, M.A./Reading Specialist

ABDO
Publishing Company

Published by ABDO Publishing Company, 8000 West 78th Street, Edina, Minnesota 55439. Copyright © 2011 by Abdo Consulting Group, Inc. International copyrights reserved in all countries. No part of this book may be reproduced in any form without written permission from the publisher. Super SandCastle™ is a trademark and logo of ABDO Publishing Company.

Printed in the United States of America, North Mankato, Minnesota
052010
092010

Editor: Katherine Hengel
Content Developer: Nancy Tuminelly
Cover and Interior Design and Production: Oona Gaarder-Juntti, Mighty Media
Photo Credits: AbleStock, iStockphoto (Denice Breaux, Sebastien Cote, Johnnyscriv, Chris Price, Sebastian Santa), Shutterstock

Library of Congress Cataloging-in-Publication Data

Gaarder-Juntti, Oona, 1979-
   What in the world is a green garden? / Oona Gaarder-Juntti.
      p. cm. -- (Going green)
   ISBN 978-1-61613-188-3
   1. Sustainable agriculture--Juvenile literature. I. Title.
S494.5.S85G33 2011
635--dc22
                                    2010004322

Super SandCastle™ books are created by a team of professional educators, reading specialists, and content developers around five essential components— phonemic awareness, phonics, vocabulary, text comprehension, and fluency— to assist young readers as they develop reading skills and strategies and increase their general knowledge. All books are written, reviewed, and leveled for guided reading, early reading intervention, and Accelerated Reader® programs for use in shared, guided, and independent reading and writing activities to support a balanced approach to literacy instruction.

ABOUT SUPER SANDCASTLE™

Bigger Books for Emerging Readers
Grades K–4

Created for library, classroom, and at-home use, Super SandCastle™ books support and engage young readers as they develop and build literacy skills and will increase their general knowledge about the world around them. Super SandCastle™ books are an extension of SandCastle™, the leading preK–3 imprint for emerging and beginning readers. Super SandCastle™ features a larger trim size for more reading fun.

Let Us Know
Super SandCastle™ would like to hear your stories about reading this book. What was your favorite page? Was there something hard that you needed help with? Share the ups and downs of learning to read. We want to hear from you! Send us an e-mail.

sandcastle@abdopublishing.com

Contact us for a complete list of SandCastle™, Super SandCastle™, and other nonfiction and fiction titles from ABDO Publishing Company.

www.abdopublishing.com • 8000 West 78th Street Edina, MN 55439 • 800-800-1312 • 952-831-1632 fax

Contents

WHAT IN THE WORLD IS BEING GREEN?

Being green means taking care of the earth. Many things on our planet are connected. When one thing changes, it can cause something else to change. That's why the way we treat the earth is so important. Keeping the earth healthy can seem like a big job. You can help by saving energy and **resources** every day.

Saving Energy

It takes energy to care for our gardens and yards! For example, lawn mowers need energy. We often burn oil for this energy. When we do, we create greenhouse gases. These gases go into the air. They can trap the sun's heat and make the earth warmer. This is called **global** warming. Saving energy reduces greenhouse gases.

Protecting Resources

Soil, trees, water, wind, and air are natural **resources**. Sometimes we waste or harm the earth's resources. For example, when we use chemicals to kill weeds, we harm the soil.

GREEN GARDENING

Gardens can be very good for the earth. They give insects and animals homes! They are good for the soil too. You can grow delicious vegetables or beautiful flowers!

Gardens are better for the earth than lawns. Growing green grass uses a lot of **resources**. You could plant a garden instead! Let's learn more about green gardens.

Did you know?

The average American throws away about 1 pound (.5 kg) of food a day.

Did you know?

5 percent of air pollution is caused by gas powered lawn mowers.

Did you know?

30 to 60 percent of fresh water is used for watering lawns and gardens.

IN A GREEN WORLD

The things we grow in our gardens can affect the earth. In a green world, we would grow things that are good for the planet!

A push lawn mower does not use gas. Using it is good exercise too!

Leaves and grass clippings make natural **fertilizers**.

Birds and insects are attracted to flowers. They help spread pollen from the flowers to other plants. Plants need pollen to grow fruits, vegetables, and seeds.

Native plants and flowers provide good homes and food for animals.

IN A GREEN WORLD

The way we care for our gardens affects the earth. In a green world, caring for our gardens would not harm the planet!

Use a **compost** bin or start a compost pile. Then you can recycle your food scraps!

Kitchen scraps can be turned into excellent **fertilizer**.

Compost reduces the amount of **fertilizer**, water, and **pesticides** needed to grow things.

A green garden provides a healthy place for birds, insects, and animals to live.

Worms like soil with compost. When they tunnel through the soil, it creates air. The air in the soil helps things grow!

HOW YOU CAN HELP

Everyone knows the 3 Rs. Reduce, Reuse, and Recycle. Do you know how to practice the 3 Rs in your garden? The next few pages will show you how! Think about what you grow and how you care for it. Think about the foods you eat and where they were grown. There are many simple ways to go green in your garden!

Trees to the Rescue!

Plants and trees keep the earth clean. They take pollution out of the air! Trees and plants also give us oxygen to breathe. Trees can save energy too. If you plant a tree by your house, it provides shade. This keeps your house cool.

1 acre (0.4 ha) of forest makes enough oxygen for 18 people for a whole year!

Veg Out!

Save a trip to the grocery store. Grow food in your backyard! Gardens need light, soil, water, and space. Ask an adult to help you find a good place.

Decide what you want to grow. You can buy seeds at a garden store, grocery store, or hardware store. Start growing your seeds in small **containers**. Try egg cartons or empty yogurt containers. The seeds will sprout into little plants called seedlings.

Loosen the soil and add **compost**. Plant your seedlings in rows. Leave plenty of room between them. They will get bigger! Remember to water and weed your new garden.

Lettuce and cherry tomatoes are easy to grow in **containers**. Make sure your containers are big enough.

Every Drop Counts

Most of the earth is covered in water. But only 1 percent of it is safe to drink. Instead of watering your garden with drinking water, use rainwater!

Rain barrels catch and store rainwater. You can buy one at a garden store. Or turn an old garbage can into a rain barrel!

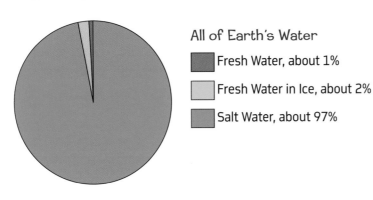

All of Earth's Water

- Fresh Water, about 1%
- Fresh Water in Ice, about 2%
- Salt Water, about 97%

Water your garden in the morning or evening when it is cool. Water **evaporates** faster when it is hot.

Don't Spray

Pesticides kill garden pests. But they can also harm humans, pets, birds, and insects. Many insects are actually good for gardens! Birds and bats are too. They like to eat the bugs that harm your garden!

Herbicides kill weeds, but they can be **toxic**. The best way to stop weeds to is to hoe and pull them out. You can also put **mulch** around your plants to stop weeds.

Mix a few drops of dish soap with water. Spray it on your plants to keep harmful bugs away!

Recycle Your Dinner

Did you know you can recycle food scraps? When food scraps rot, they become **compost**. Compost is great **fertilizer**! Start a compost pile in the corner of your yard. Or use compost bins like the ones shown on this page. Compost needs both green **matter** and brown matter. Do not add meat scraps or dairy products to your outdoor compost bins. They may attract animals!

Compost piles need air and moisture. Turn your pile every week to let in some air. Also, keep the pile moist. In a while, it will turn into excellent **fertilizer**!

Green Matter	Brown Matter
• Grass clippings	• Cardboard
• Fruit scraps	• Leaves
• Vegetable scraps	• Newspapers
• Coffee grounds	• Twigs
• Tea bags	• Sawdust
• Egg shells	• Paper napkins

LET'S THINK GREEN

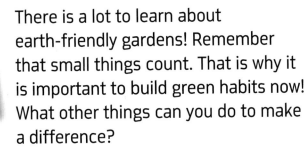

There is a lot to learn about earth-friendly gardens! Remember that small things count. That is why it is important to build green habits now! What other things can you do to make a difference?

Taking care of the earth is everyone's responsibility. That means kids and adults! Talk with your family and friends about green gardens. Let's all work hard together and think green!

TAKE THE GREEN PLEDGE

I promise to help the earth every day by doing things in a different way.

In the garden I can help by:

♻ Growing more native plants and flowers.

♻ **Composting** my food scraps.

♻ Watering my garden with rainwater.

♻ Eating less packaged food and growing my own.

GLOSSARY

compost – a mixture of natural materials, such as food scraps and lawn clippings, that can turn into fertilizer over time.

container – something that other things can be put into.

evaporate – to change from a liquid to a gas.

fertilizer – something used to make plants grow better in soil.

global – having to do with the whole earth.

herbicide – a chemical used to stop plants from growing.

matter – anything that takes up space or has weight.

mulch – something, such as straw or wood chips, spread over the ground to protect plants.

pesticide – a chemical used to kill pests.

preservative – a chemical added to food to keep it from spoiling or changing color.

resource – the supply or source of something. A *natural resource* is a resource found in nature, such as water or trees.

toxic – containing something that can injure or kill.